Chapter 1: A New Dawn

The rumble of Lisa's station wagon filled the quiet highway as she drove into the unknown, her knuckles pale as she gripped the wheel. The faint scent of leather mixed with the remnants of a fast-food meal the kids had half-eaten earlier. She had driven for hours with no clear destination, only one goal: to leave behind the suffocating darkness of her past.

The bruises on her arm ached faintly, a cruel reminder of why she was here. Beside her, the California sun was beginning to dip low, the horizon washed in gold and deep orange. Her eyes burned, but she couldn't cry. Not yet.

"Mommy?" Mia's soft voice piped up from the backseat. Lisa glanced over her shoulder, meeting her daughter's wide, sleepy eyes.

"Yes, baby?"

"Where are we going?"

"To a better place," Lisa said, forcing a smile. "A safer place."

Mia blinked, then turned over to snuggle into her brother, Kyle, who was snoring softly.

Lisa exhaled shakily, her chest tightening with guilt. How had she let it go on so long? The yelling, the bruises, the way her husband had chipped away at her soul piece by piece. She had stayed for the children, she told herself, but deep down she knew fear had been her greatest captor.

Ahead, a green sign announced the town of Willow Creek. Population: 4,312. Lisa slowed the car as the main street came into view. A string of small shops lined one side of the road, their windows dimly lit. The other side had a diner, a pharmacy, and a hardware store. It wasn't much, but it looked peaceful, quaint.

"This will do," Lisa murmured, pulling up in front of a white house with a sagging porch. The rental agent had assured her it was "cozy" and "affordable," which Lisa took to mean old and small.

The house smelled faintly of dust and lemons when they stepped inside. The wooden floors creaked underfoot, and the walls were bare except for a few cobwebs in the corners.

"Is this home now?" Kyle asked, his voice groggy.

"Yes," Lisa said, kneeling to meet his eyes. She smoothed his unruly curls and kissed his forehead. "This is our home."

The kids wandered off to explore the small bedrooms while Lisa stood in the living room, taking in her new reality. She had no furniture yet, just a few bags of clothes, an air mattress, and a box of kitchen essentials. But for the first time in years, she felt something akin to hope.

That night, after the kids were asleep on the air mattress, Lisa sat on the porch steps with a glass of water, staring at the stars. The quiet was almost deafening compared to the chaos she'd left behind. A light breeze brushed her skin, and for the first time in a long time, she allowed herself to dream of a better future.

"I'll get through this," she whispered to herself. "One step at a time."

Chapter 2: Adjusting to Willow Creek

The next morning, sunlight streamed through the cracked blinds, waking Lisa before her alarm. The house felt eerily quiet without the usual tension of walking on eggshells around her husband. She padded into the kitchen and started a pot of coffee, letting the rich aroma fill the air.

Her first task was to settle into Willow Creek. She dropped the kids off at their new school, a red-brick building that looked more like a church than an elementary school. Mia clung to her leg, hesitant to let go, but Kyle tugged his sister's hand.

"We'll be fine, Mom," Kyle said, his confidence surprising Lisa.

As she drove to the local grocery store, Lisa made a mental list of everything she needed: cleaning supplies, food, maybe a few plants to brighten up the house. She parked her car and stepped into the store, immediately feeling the eyes of a few locals on her.

"New in town?" The cashier, a gray-haired woman with a warm smile, asked as Lisa unloaded her items onto the conveyor belt.

"Yeah," Lisa said, forcing a polite smile. "Just moved here with my kids."

"Welcome to Willow Creek. Folks around here are friendly—just holler if you need anything."

Lisa nodded, appreciating the kindness but unsure if she was ready to trust anyone just yet.

Later, as she scrubbed the kitchen counters and unpacked boxes, Lisa felt a flicker of determination. This was her fresh start, and she was determined to make the most of it.

Chapter 3: Flashbacks and Fresh Wounds

The morning sun spilled golden light across the modest kitchen table as Lisa sat with her coffee, staring at the bills spread out before her. The house was still quiet; Mia and Kyle were likely still asleep. It had been a week since they'd moved into the house, and though the small town offered her a sense of calm, it hadn't done much to silence the memories.

Lisa rubbed her temples, trying to shake the image that had invaded her dreams last night—her ex-husband, Marcus, towering over her, his voice loud and cruel as he berated her for forgetting to iron his shirt.

"I'm not there anymore," she whispered to herself, gripping her mug tightly. "I'm safe now."

But safety didn't stop the flood of memories. Marcus had been charming when they first met—a sweet-talking, handsome man with a wide smile that had drawn her in like a moth to a flame. She was young and eager for love, ready to believe in fairy tales. But the fairy tale had turned dark quickly.

Her phone buzzed, jolting her out of the past. She reached for it hesitantly, a chill running down her spine when she saw Marcus's name flash on the screen. For a moment, she froze, her pulse quickening.

No. She wasn't going to let him control her anymore. With trembling hands, she blocked the number and set the phone down, her breath coming in short gasps.

Later that day, Lisa took the kids to the park down the street. Willow Creek's park wasn't anything fancy—a wooden playground set, a couple of picnic tables, and a small pond surrounded by weeping willows. But it was enough for Kyle and Mia, who ran off to explore as soon as they arrived.

Lisa settled onto a bench, the breeze carrying the faint scent of blooming jasmine. She watched her children laughing and chasing each other, their joy a stark contrast to the tension-filled home they'd come from. For the first time in years, they looked like kids who didn't have a care in the world.

A woman with auburn curls and a friendly smile approached Lisa, carrying a Tupperware container. "Hi, you must be new here. I'm Maggie."

Lisa hesitated, her instinct to keep people at arm's length kicking in. But Maggie's open demeanor softened her defenses. "Hi, I'm Lisa," she said, shaking Maggie's hand.

"Welcome to Willow Creek," Maggie said, handing her the container. "I made some banana bread. It's a little tradition of mine for new neighbors."

Lisa accepted the container, feeling a lump form in her throat. It had been so long since someone had done something kind for her without expecting anything in return.

"Thank you," Lisa said, her voice barely above a whisper.

Maggie sat beside her, watching the kids play. "It's a nice town, you'll see. Quiet, but nice. What brought you here?"

Lisa hesitated, unsure how much to reveal. "Just needed a fresh start," she said finally.

Maggie nodded, as if she understood more than Lisa had said. "Well, if you ever need anything, I live a few houses down from you. The one with the blue shutters."

That night, after the kids were asleep, Lisa found herself staring at the container of banana bread on the counter. She cut a slice, savoring the warm, comforting flavor. It reminded her of childhood, of the rare moments when life had felt simple.

She allowed herself a small smile, realizing she'd made it through another day. One day at a time—that's how she'd get through this.

Understood! I'll dedicate the next chapters to Lisa's personal healing—unpacking her trauma, building relationships with her children, and finding her footing in Willow Creek. Here's **Chapter 4**:

Chapter 4: Pieces of Herself

The days in Willow Creek began to blend together in a slow, steady rhythm. Lisa woke early to make breakfast, drove the kids to school, and spent her afternoons tidying the house or walking through the quiet streets. It wasn't much, but the peace of the routine felt like salve on an open wound.

One crisp morning, Lisa decided to visit the local thrift shop. The house felt too empty, and she figured filling it with a few personal touches might make it feel more like home.

The thrift shop was tucked between a bakery and an antique store. Its weathered sign read "Second Chances," and Lisa smiled wryly at the name.

Inside, the air smelled of old books and lavender sachets. Shelves were crammed with mismatched dishes, faded quilts, and picture frames. Lisa wandered through the aisles, running her fingers over the trinkets and treasures.

She stopped at a shelf of books and picked up a worn copy of *The Bluest Eye* by Toni Morrison. The pages were soft and dog-eared, as though someone had loved it deeply. She added it to her basket along with a small vase and a framed painting of a willow tree.

That evening, Lisa set the vase on the kitchen table and placed the painting above the fireplace. She stood back, hands on her hips, and smiled faintly. It wasn't much, but it was a start.

Later, she curled up on the couch with the book, its opening lines pulling her into another world. She read until her eyes grew heavy, feeling a flicker of something she hadn't felt in a long time—contentment.

Flashbacks in the Night
The contentment didn't last long. That night, Lisa woke in a cold sweat, Marcus's voice echoing in her ears.

"You're worthless, Lisa. You'll never be anything without me."

She sat up, gasping for breath. Her chest felt tight, and tears streamed down her cheeks. The nightmares had become less frequent since the move, but when they came, they left her shaken for days.

Lisa swung her legs over the side of the bed and padded into the kitchen. She poured herself a glass of water and leaned against the counter, staring out the window at the dark street.

"Why can't I let it go?" she whispered to herself.

She thought of her children, how she was trying to be strong for them. But on nights like this, the weight of her past felt unbearable.

Small Steps Forward

The next morning, Lisa decided to try something new. She found an old notebook buried in a moving box and began writing. At first, the words came slowly, each one dredged up from the depths of her pain. But soon, the pen moved faster, spilling her thoughts onto the page.

Dear Marcus, she wrote. *You told me I was nothing. You told me I was weak. But you were wrong. I'm stronger than you ever gave me credit for.*

Tears blurred her vision, but she kept writing, pouring out years of anger, hurt, and frustration. When she finished, she felt lighter, as though a small piece of her burden had been lifted.

Lisa closed the notebook and set it on the nightstand. She wasn't ready to let go of the past entirely, but writing felt like the first step toward healing.

A Day at the Beach

That weekend, Lisa took the kids to the beach. The Pacific Ocean stretched out before them, its waves crashing against the shore in a soothing rhythm.

Mia squealed with delight as she chased seagulls, while Kyle built a sandcastle with serious determination. Lisa watched them, a soft smile tugging at her lips.

For the first time in years, she felt a flicker of hope.

Chapter 5: Opening Doors

The sun was just beginning to rise when Lisa stepped outside with her cup of coffee. The porch was becoming her sanctuary, a quiet place where she could gather her thoughts before the day began. This morning, the air was crisp, carrying the scent of dew and wildflowers.

She watched as a group of joggers passed by on the sidewalk, their rhythmic footsteps echoing in the stillness. They waved, and Lisa hesitated for a moment before lifting her hand in return.

Maybe this is what healing looks like, she thought. Little moments of connection, even if they felt foreign.

Unexpected Visitors
Later that day, as Lisa was unpacking a box of books in the living room, there was a knock at the door. She hesitated, her heart quickening. Visitors were rare, and her first instinct was to pretend she wasn't home.

But then she thought of Maggie, her kind neighbor who had brought over banana bread. She exhaled and opened the door.

Standing on the porch was an older man with a weathered face and kind eyes. He wore overalls and carried a basket filled with peaches.

"Afternoon," he said, tipping his hat. "Name's Earl. I live two doors down. Figured you might like some fresh peaches. Got a tree that produces more than I can eat."

Lisa blinked, taken aback by the gesture. "Oh, thank you. That's very kind."

Earl grinned. "No trouble at all. Welcome to the neighborhood." He glanced past her shoulder at the boxes scattered around the living room. "Looks like you're still settling in. If you need anything, just holler."

"I will," Lisa said, offering a small smile.

As Earl left, Lisa closed the door and stared at the basket of peaches. It was such a small thing, but it warmed her heart. People here were different—kinder, gentler. Maybe she could get used to this.

A New Routine

Over the next few weeks, Lisa fell into a steady routine. She spent her mornings journaling, her afternoons exploring the town, and her evenings with Kyle and Mia.

She started visiting the library, a cozy building with creaky wooden floors and shelves that smelled of old paper. The librarian, a petite woman named Clara, always greeted her warmly and recommended books for her and the kids.

One day, as Lisa was checking out a stack of novels, Clara leaned over the counter. "You should come to the book club we host here on Thursday nights. It's small, but we have a good time."

Lisa hesitated. The idea of sitting in a room full of strangers made her palms sweat. But Clara's enthusiasm was contagious, and Lisa found herself nodding. "Maybe I'll stop by."

Book Club Night

Thursday arrived faster than Lisa expected. She stood in front of the mirror, smoothing down the front of her blouse. It felt strange to dress up, even just a little.

"Are you going out, Mom?" Mia asked, peeking into the room.

Lisa smiled. "Just to a book club at the library."

Mia tilted her head. "Will there be other moms there?"

"Probably," Lisa said, laughing softly. "Why?"

Mia shrugged. "I think it's good. You need friends."

Lisa's smile faltered. Out of the mouths of babes.

The book club was small, just six people gathered around a table in the library's reading room. Lisa felt awkward at first, her gaze darting around the room as the others introduced themselves.

But as the discussion began, she found herself relaxing. They were reading *Their Eyes Were Watching God* by Zora Neale Hurston, and the group's thoughtful insights made Lisa feel like part of something bigger. By the end of the night, she was laughing along with the others, a warm feeling spreading in her chest.

A Letter to Herself
That night, Lisa sat on her bed with her notebook open. But instead of writing to Marcus, she decided to write to herself.

Dear Lisa, she began. *You've been through hell, but you're still standing. You're stronger than you think, even if it doesn't feel like it. Keep going. You deserve happiness.*

She closed the notebook and set it on the nightstand, a single tear slipping down her cheek. For the first time, she believed her own words.

Chapter 6: Foundations of Trust

The days in Willow Creek were beginning to feel like a life Lisa could settle into. Her once-frequent nightmares had grown less vivid, and her journal was filling with pages of thoughts she hadn't been brave enough to face until now.

Morning Walks

One quiet morning, Lisa decided to take a walk after dropping the kids off at school. The town had a charm she hadn't noticed when she first arrived—colorful flower boxes beneath windows, handwritten signs in shopfronts, and the soft murmur of greetings exchanged between neighbors.

Lisa followed a gravel path that wound through the park and ended at a small pond. She stopped to watch the ducks, their movements serene and unhurried. The simplicity of the moment calmed her in a way she hadn't expected.

"Lovely morning, isn't it?"

Lisa turned to see Maggie standing a few feet away, holding a leash attached to a small, scruffy dog.

"It is," Lisa replied, smiling softly.

Maggie motioned to the bench nearby. "Mind if I join you?"

Lisa hesitated for only a second before nodding.

The two women sat in silence for a moment, the dog curling up at Maggie's feet.

"How are you settling in?" Maggie asked, her tone casual but kind.

"It's... different," Lisa admitted. "Quiet, but good. The kids are adjusting well."

"And you?" Maggie tilted her head, her auburn curls catching the sunlight.

Lisa sighed, a small but genuine smile tugging at her lips. "I'm getting there. One step at a time."

Maggie patted her knee. "That's all any of us can do."

Building Connections

The conversation with Maggie gave Lisa a small boost of confidence. Over the next few weeks, she started to open up more—to her neighbors, to the librarian Clara, and even to the parents she met while waiting to pick up her kids.

At first, the interactions felt forced, her responses clipped and cautious. But as she grew more comfortable, she found herself laughing at jokes and sharing bits of her life. She didn't mention Marcus or the abuse, but she began to talk about her love of books, her childhood in Oakland, and her dreams of one day starting her own small business.

The Garden
One afternoon, Lisa decided to tackle the neglected backyard. The patchy grass and overgrown weeds felt like a metaphor for her life—messy but full of potential.

She spent hours pulling weeds, her hands blistered and her back aching. But as she worked, she felt a sense of accomplishment she hadn't felt in years. By the time the sun began to set, she had cleared a small space for a garden.

Mia and Kyle came outside, their eyes lighting up when they saw the cleared patch of earth.

"What are you going to plant, Mom?" Mia asked, her voice full of curiosity.

"I'm not sure yet," Lisa admitted, brushing dirt off her hands. "What do you two think?"

"Strawberries!" Mia said, clapping her hands.

"Tomatoes," Kyle added, his tone more practical.

Lisa laughed, the sound surprising her. "Alright, strawberries and tomatoes it is."

Letters and Reflections
That night, Lisa wrote in her journal again. This time, she wrote about the garden.

Today felt like a new beginning. I know it's just a patch of dirt, but it's mine. It's ours. And maybe, just maybe, it's a sign that I'm ready to grow, too.

As she closed the notebook, Lisa felt a flicker of pride. She still had a long way to go, but for the first time, she felt like she was moving forward.

A Glimpse of Harlo

The next morning, as Lisa was leaving the grocery store, she bumped into someone near the entrance.

"Oh, I'm sorry," she said, looking up.

The man standing before her was tall and broad-shouldered, with kind eyes that crinkled slightly when he smiled.

"No harm done," he said, his voice deep and gentle. "I should've been paying more attention."

Lisa nodded, feeling a bit flustered. She stepped aside to let him pass, but he paused.

"Are you new in town?" he asked, his tone friendly.

Lisa hesitated before answering. "Yes. Just moved here with my kids."

"Well, welcome. I'm Harlo," he said, offering his hand.

"Lisa," she replied, shaking his hand briefly.

Harlo smiled again before stepping into the store, leaving Lisa standing in the doorway, her heart unexpectedly racing.

Got it! I'll weave Lisa's healing journey with her growing interactions with Harlo, keeping the pace natural and heartfelt as Lisa begins to explore the possibility of love while continuing to build herself up. Here's **Chapter 7**:

Chapter 7: Seeds of Trust

The days passed like a soft melody, one note blending into the next. Lisa spent her mornings tending to the small garden in her backyard. She had planted strawberries, tomatoes, and a few wildflowers, and the act of nurturing something alive gave her a quiet sense of fulfillment.

But her encounter with Harlo lingered in her mind. His kind eyes and gentle demeanor were a stark contrast to the men she'd known in the past. She hadn't expected such a simple interaction to leave an impression, but it had.

A Chance Meeting
One Saturday afternoon, Lisa and the kids walked to the local farmer's market. Stalls lined the town square, filled with fresh produce, handmade crafts, and baked goods.

As Mia and Kyle darted ahead to look at a booth selling honey, Lisa wandered to a stand selling potted herbs. She was inspecting a basil plant when a familiar voice spoke behind her.

"Good choice. Basil's easy to grow, and it smells great in the kitchen."

Lisa turned to see Harlo standing there, holding a basket of vegetables. He was dressed in a casual plaid shirt, his sleeves rolled up to reveal strong forearms.

"Oh, hi," Lisa said, feeling a little caught off guard. "I didn't expect to see you here."

Harlo chuckled. "I'm here every week. Best place to get fresh produce."

Lisa nodded, suddenly unsure of what to say.

"Do you garden?" Harlo asked, gesturing to the basil plant.

"Sort of," Lisa replied. "I just started a small one in my backyard. It's... therapeutic."

Harlo smiled, his expression warm. "I know what you mean. I've got a little plot at home too. Nothing fancy, but it keeps me busy."

They talked for a few more minutes, their conversation light and easy. When Mia and Kyle ran over with sticky fingers and wide smiles, Harlo greeted them kindly, introducing himself without hesitation.

As they walked home, Lisa realized she was smiling—a real, unforced smile that lingered even as the sun began to set.

Hesitation and Reflection
That evening, Lisa sat on the porch with her journal. She hadn't written much about Harlo, but tonight, she found herself reflecting on their conversation.

He's kind. It's strange how much that stands out to me. I don't know if I'm ready for anything more than casual conversations, but it's nice to talk to someone who doesn't make me feel small.

She closed the journal and leaned back in her chair, staring up at the stars. Part of her longed to open herself up to the possibility of love, but another part was terrified.

A Neighborly Gesture
A week later, Lisa was kneeling in the garden, pulling weeds, when she heard a knock on the fence. She looked up to see Harlo standing there, holding a tray of seedlings.

"I heard you've got a garden," he said, smiling. "Thought you might like these. They're peppers—easy to grow, and they add a little spice to life."

Lisa stood, brushing dirt from her hands. "That's thoughtful of you. Thank you."

Harlo handed her the tray, his smile never wavering. "It's no trouble. Let me know if you need any tips. I've been gardening for years."

Lisa hesitated, then said, "Would you like some lemonade? I just made a fresh batch."

Harlo nodded. "I'd like that."

They sat on the porch, sipping lemonade and talking about everything from gardening to the quirks of small-town life. Harlo told her about his job as a carpenter and how he'd ended up in Willow Creek after years of traveling.

"Settling down here felt right," he said. "It's a good place to find peace."

Lisa nodded, understanding more than she let on.

A Spark of Connection
Over the next few weeks, Harlo became a regular presence in Lisa's life. He stopped by to check on her garden, offered to fix the squeaky gate in her backyard, and even helped Kyle build a birdhouse for a school project.

Lisa found herself looking forward to his visits, but she also felt the familiar tug of fear. Letting someone in meant risking pain, and she wasn't sure if she was ready for that.

One evening, as they sat on the porch watching the fireflies, Harlo turned to her and said, "You're strong, Lisa. I can see it in the way you carry yourself, in the way you care for your kids. But you don't have to do it all alone."

His words hit her like a gentle wave, both soothing and unsettling. She wanted to believe him, but trust didn't come easily.

Planting Seeds of Trust
That night, Lisa wrote in her journal again.

I don't know what's happening with Harlo. Maybe it's just friendship. Maybe it's more. But for the first time in years, I feel like I can breathe around someone. That has to count for something.

She set the notebook aside and climbed into bed, her heart both heavy and light.

Chapter 8: A Growing Friendship

Harlo's presence in Lisa's life became a constant, a steady rhythm that added warmth to her days. It wasn't overwhelming or intrusive—he had a way of simply being there when she needed him, even if she didn't realize it herself.

A Surprise Dinner
One evening, Lisa came home from work to find a note taped to her front door. The handwriting was neat and deliberate.

Hope you like chili. Come by if you're hungry. —Harlo

Lisa stared at the note, her emotions swirling. It had been years since anyone had cooked for her without expecting something in return. She glanced at her kids, who were already reading over her shoulder.

"Chili sounds good, Mom," Kyle said, his tone hopeful.

Mia nodded. "He seems nice."

Lisa sighed, a reluctant smile creeping onto her face. "Alright, let's go."

Harlo's house was just a few streets away, a modest but well-kept home with a wraparound porch. When they arrived, he greeted them with a wide smile, his apron smeared with evidence of his cooking efforts.

"Come on in," he said, holding the door open.

The house smelled amazing—spices mingling with the aroma of slow-cooked meat. The table was set with mismatched dishes, and a pitcher of iced tea sat in the center.

"I hope you're hungry," Harlo said, ladling chili into bowls.

As they ate, the conversation flowed easily. Harlo asked Kyle about his favorite school subjects and listened attentively as Mia recounted a funny story about her teacher. Lisa watched from the sidelines, marveling at how naturally her children had taken to him.

After dinner, Harlo brought out a plate of cookies and challenged the kids to a game of checkers. Lisa stayed back, sipping her tea and taking it all in.

For the first time in years, she felt like her family was whole again.

The Dance Hall
The following weekend, Harlo stopped by with an unusual suggestion.

"There's a dance hall in town," he said. "They're having live music tomorrow night. Thought you might want to come along."

Lisa raised an eyebrow. "Dancing?"

Harlo shrugged. "Doesn't have to be dancing. Could just be listening to the music, enjoying the company. No pressure."

Lisa hesitated. The idea of stepping into a social situation felt daunting, but the thought of staying home alone felt worse.

"Alright," she said finally. "But don't expect me to dance."

The dance hall was buzzing with life when they arrived. Strings of lights hung from the rafters, casting a warm glow over the crowd. A band played in the corner, their music a mix of country and blues.

Lisa stayed near the edge of the room, sipping her drink and watching Harlo chat with a few locals. He seemed to know everyone, his easygoing nature making him the center of attention without even trying.

Eventually, he made his way back to her.

"Enjoying yourself?" he asked.

"It's... nice," Lisa admitted.

Harlo grinned. "Come on, one dance won't kill you."

Lisa shook her head, laughing softly. "I told you, I don't dance."

"Sure you do," Harlo said, holding out his hand. "You just haven't in a while."

His words struck a chord, and after a moment's hesitation, Lisa placed her hand in his.

The music was slow, the kind that made you sway more than step. Harlo guided her gently, his hand steady on her waist. Lisa felt awkward at first, her body stiff and unyielding.

"Relax," Harlo said, his voice low. "Just follow my lead."

And she did. For the first time in years, Lisa let herself be vulnerable. The world around them blurred as they moved together, the music carrying them along.

Quiet Conversations
On the walk home, the air was cool and crisp. Lisa pulled her jacket tighter around her, her mind still buzzing from the night's events.

"Thank you," she said softly.

"For what?" Harlo asked.

"For... everything," Lisa replied. "For being patient. For not pushing."

Harlo stopped and turned to her. "Lisa, I'm not here to rush you into anything. I just like spending time with you. That's enough for me."

His words were simple, but they carried a weight that made Lisa's chest tighten.

"I'm trying," she said, her voice barely above a whisper.

"I know," Harlo replied. "And that's more than enough."

A Night of Reflection
That night, Lisa sat on her porch with her journal. She didn't write much, just a single sentence.

Maybe it's okay to let someone in again.

She closed the notebook and leaned back, staring up at the stars. For the first time in a long time, she felt something other than fear. She felt hope.

Chapter 9: The Walls Within

Lisa woke up the next morning feeling lighter than she had in years. The evening with Harlo had been nothing short of magical, but as the day wore on, that familiar voice of doubt crept back in.

Morning Shadows
Sitting at the kitchen table with a cup of coffee, Lisa stared out the window at her garden. The strawberries were beginning to flower, and the sight should have brought her joy. Instead, a heavy sense of unease settled in her chest.

"What am I doing?" she muttered to herself.

Her mind raced with thoughts she couldn't quiet. What if she let Harlo in and it all fell apart? What if he turned out to be someone she couldn't trust? She had been wrong before—terribly wrong—and the stakes felt higher now, with her children and her own fragile sense of self-worth on the line.

A Triggering Reminder
That afternoon, Lisa took Mia and Kyle shopping in the next town over. As they walked through the aisles of the grocery store, Lisa spotted a man who bore an uncanny resemblance to Marcus.

Her heart stopped.

The man's build, the way he walked, even the tilt of his head—it all brought back a flood of memories she'd tried so hard to bury. She froze in place, her breath shallow and her hands trembling.

"Mom?" Kyle's voice broke through the haze.

Lisa turned to her son, her eyes wide and unfocused. "What?"

"Are you okay?" he asked, concern etched on his young face.

Lisa forced a smile, though it felt more like a grimace. "I'm fine. Let's just... let's go home."

A Talk with Maggie
Back in Willow Creek, Lisa stopped by Maggie's house. She hadn't planned to, but as she drove past, she saw Maggie tending to her roses and felt a pull to stop.

"You look like you've seen a ghost," Maggie said as Lisa stepped out of the car.

Lisa managed a weak laugh. "Something like that."

They sat on Maggie's porch, sipping sweet tea. Lisa recounted what had happened at the store, her voice shaky.

"It wasn't him, but it didn't matter," Lisa admitted. "For a moment, I felt like I was back there. Back in that house. Back in that life."

Maggie reached over and squeezed her hand. "You've come so far, Lisa. Those feelings—those memories—they're going to creep up on you from time to time. But they don't define who you are now."

Lisa nodded, though her chest still felt tight. "It's just hard. Letting go of the past, trusting that things can be different."

Maggie smiled gently. "You don't have to let go all at once. Just loosen your grip a little."

A Moment of Doubt
That evening, Harlo stopped by with a bag of freshly baked bread from the local bakery.

"I figured you might like this," he said, handing it to her with an easy smile.

"Thanks," Lisa said, her voice quieter than usual.

Harlo tilted his head. "You alright?"

Lisa hesitated, then shook her head. "It's nothing. Just... a rough day."

Harlo studied her for a moment but didn't press. "Well, if you want to talk, you know where to find me."

Lisa nodded, watching as he walked away. Part of her wanted to call him back, to open up and let him in. But another part—the part that had been burned before—kept her rooted in place.

The Breakdown

Later that night, Lisa sat in the living room after the kids had gone to bed. A glass of wine sat untouched on the table, and the only sound was the ticking of the clock on the wall.

Her emotions bubbled to the surface, a storm she could no longer contain. She buried her face in her hands, tears streaming down her cheeks.

"I can't do this," she whispered to herself. "I can't go through this again."

But as the tears fell, something shifted. She thought about her garden, about the dance hall, about Harlo's steady presence.

Maybe she couldn't do it alone, but did she have to?

A Small Step Forward

The next day, Lisa made a decision. She walked to Harlo's house, her heart pounding with every step.

When he opened the door, his expression shifted from surprise to concern.

"Lisa? Is everything okay?"

Lisa took a deep breath, forcing herself to meet his eyes. "No," she said honestly. "But I want to try. I want to try to let you in."

Harlo stepped aside, motioning for her to come in. "We'll take it slow," he said softly. "Whatever pace you need."

Lisa nodded, her chest still tight but her resolve firm. For the first time, she felt like she was choosing herself—choosing her healing, her happiness, and maybe even the possibility of love.

Chapter 10: Building Bridges

The days that followed Lisa's decision to let Harlo in were both challenging and rewarding. Every interaction with him felt like a small step toward something she hadn't dared to hope for: a life where she could be herself without fear of judgment or pain.

But it wasn't without its struggles. Trust, Lisa realized, wasn't something she could switch on like a light. It was built slowly, layer by layer.

An Afternoon in the Garden
One sunny afternoon, Harlo stopped by unannounced, carrying a small wooden crate.

"What's that?" Lisa asked, wiping her hands on her jeans.

"Garden tools," Harlo said with a grin. "Thought I'd help you with those weeds."

Lisa raised an eyebrow. "Are you saying my garden's a mess?"

Harlo chuckled. "Not at all. I'm saying even the best gardens need a little teamwork."

Lisa couldn't argue with that. Together, they knelt in the dirt, pulling weeds and turning the soil. Harlo showed her a trick for planting herbs in a way that would keep them from overcrowding, his hands steady as he demonstrated.

"You're good at this," Lisa said, glancing at him.

Harlo shrugged. "I've always liked working with my hands. Gardening, carpentry—it's all about creating something from nothing."

Lisa nodded, feeling a sense of peace she hadn't experienced in years.

As they worked, their conversation flowed effortlessly. Harlo told her stories about his childhood and the small woodworking shop he'd started in town. Lisa shared bits and pieces of her life, careful not to reveal too much but still letting him in a little more each time.

A Rainy Afternoon Indoors
A week later, a sudden downpour kept Lisa and the kids cooped up inside. Harlo showed up with a board game tucked under his arm.

"I figured you might need some entertainment," he said, shaking the rain from his coat.

Kyle's eyes lit up. "Is that *Monopoly*?"

"It sure is," Harlo replied.

The game quickly became a chaotic affair. Kyle was ruthless, buying up properties and charging exorbitant rent, while Mia giggled every time she landed on Free Parking.

Lisa found herself laughing more than she had in months, especially when Harlo kept landing on her hotels.

"You're killing me, Lisa," Harlo said, pretending to clutch his chest as he handed over his last few dollars.

"You should've bought Boardwalk when you had the chance," Lisa teased, a sly smile on her face.

By the time the game ended, the storm had passed, and so had another invisible barrier between them.

A Quiet Walk

One evening, Harlo suggested they take a walk. The air was cool, and the streets were quiet as they strolled through the town.

"I like this time of day," Harlo said. "Everything feels... calm."

Lisa nodded. "It's nice. Peaceful."

As they walked, Harlo glanced at her. "Can I ask you something?"

Lisa hesitated but nodded.

"What scares you the most about letting someone in?" he asked gently.

Lisa stopped walking, her heart pounding. She looked down at the pavement, struggling to find the words.

"Losing myself," she said finally. "I gave so much of myself in the past, and it... it broke me. I don't think I could survive that again."

Harlo was silent for a moment, then said, "I get that. But you're not the same person you were back then. You're stronger now. You know your worth."

Lisa met his gaze, her eyes shimmering with unshed tears. "It's hard to believe that sometimes."

"Well," Harlo said with a small smile, "then let me remind you."

A Step Closer

The next time Harlo stopped by, he brought a small wooden box. Inside was a handcrafted birdhouse, its design intricate and thoughtful.

"I made this for your garden," he said, setting it on the porch. "Thought it could use a little extra charm."

Lisa ran her fingers over the smooth wood, her throat tightening. "It's beautiful," she said softly. "Thank you."

Harlo shrugged, his cheeks tinged with the faintest blush. "It's nothing, really."

But it wasn't nothing to Lisa. It was a gesture of care, of someone who saw her and wanted to give her something meaningful.

Later, as they hung the birdhouse together, Lisa felt a sense of warmth she hadn't known in years.

Small Moments of Joy
Over the weeks, Lisa and Harlo continued to build their connection through small moments. They cooked together, swapped books, and spent quiet evenings on the porch, talking about everything and nothing.

Harlo never pushed, never demanded more than Lisa was ready to give. And in that space of patience and respect, Lisa found herself beginning to trust—not just him, but her own ability to choose someone good.

The First Touch
One evening, as they sat on the porch watching the sunset, Harlo reached over and took Lisa's hand.

The gesture was so simple, yet it sent a wave of emotion through her.

Lisa didn't pull away. Instead, she let herself sit with the feeling, the warmth of his hand in hers.

"I'm scared," she admitted, her voice barely above a whisper.

"I know," Harlo said. "But you don't have to face it alone."

In that moment, Lisa realized she didn't feel alone. For the first time in years, she felt like someone was standing beside her, not to control or fix her, but to support her as she rebuilt herself.

And for now, that was enough.

Chapter 11: The Pivotal Moment

The day started like any other, with Lisa tending to her garden and preparing for work. The sun was warm, the sky a perfect shade of blue, and a gentle breeze carried the scent of lavender from the bushes lining her yard.

She felt a quiet contentment that had become increasingly familiar in Harlo's presence. But life, as Lisa knew all too well, had a way of throwing curveballs just when things seemed to settle.

An Unexpected Visit
Lisa was at the local diner later that afternoon, picking up a pie for dessert, when she spotted a man walking toward her. Her blood ran cold. It was Marcus.

Her ex-husband.

He hadn't changed much. His tall frame was as imposing as ever, his sharp features marked by a smug expression she remembered too well.

"Lisa," he said, stopping in front of her.

Her chest tightened. "What are you doing here, Marcus?"

"I came to see you," he said, his voice low but insistent. "We need to talk."

"There's nothing to talk about," Lisa said, her voice steadier than she felt.

"Don't be like that," Marcus replied, taking a step closer. "I've changed. I want to make things right."

Lisa's hands trembled as she clutched the pie box. Memories of their life together flashed through her mind: the shouting, the manipulation, the bruises she'd hidden from the world.

Before she could respond, Harlo's voice cut through the tension.

"Everything alright here?"

Lisa turned to see Harlo standing a few feet away, his posture calm but his eyes sharp as they locked onto Marcus.

Marcus sneered. "Who's this?"

"I'm Harlo," he said simply, stepping closer to Lisa. "A friend."

Marcus looked Harlo up and down, his smirk fading. "You think you can just replace me?"

Lisa found her voice then, stronger this time. "Marcus, leave. Now."

For a moment, it seemed like Marcus might push back, but the quiet strength in Harlo's stance—and Lisa's unwavering gaze—made him think twice. With a muttered curse, he turned and walked away.

The Fallout
Back at Lisa's house, Harlo stayed silent as she paced the living room, her emotions a whirlwind.

"He has no right to show up here," Lisa said, her voice shaking. "After everything he did—after everything I've been through."

Harlo sat on the couch, his expression calm but concerned. "You don't have to explain anything to me," he said gently.

Lisa stopped pacing and turned to him. "I feel like I've been doing so well, and then he shows up, and it's like I'm back to being that scared, helpless woman."

"You're not that woman anymore," Harlo said, his tone firm. "You stood up to him, Lisa. That's not something you could've done back then."

His words sank in, and Lisa felt a wave of gratitude mixed with exhaustion. She sat down beside him, her hands still trembling.

"I hate that he still has this power over me," she admitted.

Harlo reached for her hand, holding it gently. "The only power he has is what you give him. And from where I'm sitting, you didn't give him much."

Lisa looked at him, her eyes brimming with tears. "I don't know what I'd do without you."

Harlo smiled softly. "You'd be just fine, Lisa. But I'm glad I'm here."

A Moment of Vulnerability

That evening, after the kids were in bed, Lisa found Harlo still sitting on the porch. He'd stayed longer than usual, sensing she needed the extra support.

She brought out two mugs of tea and sat beside him.

"I'm sorry for dragging you into that," she said.

"You didn't drag me into anything," Harlo replied. "I'm here because I want to be."

Lisa hesitated, then said, "When Marcus was around, I felt so small. Like I didn't matter. And for a long time, I thought that was all I deserved."

"You deserve so much more than that," Harlo said, his voice steady.

Lisa looked at him, her heart aching with a mix of fear and hope. "I don't know if I can ever be the person you deserve."

Harlo reached over, tucking a stray strand of hair behind her ear. "Lisa, I'm not asking you to be anyone but yourself. That's all I want."

The tenderness in his voice broke down her remaining walls. For the first time, she leaned into him, letting herself be held.

And for the first time, she didn't feel weak for needing someone. She felt human.

The First Kiss
As the night deepened and the stars filled the sky, Lisa and Harlo sat in comfortable silence.

Lisa tilted her head up to look at him. "Thank you," she said softly.

"For what?"

"For being patient. For not giving up on me."

Harlo smiled, his gaze warm and steady. "You're worth it, Lisa."

In that moment, something shifted. Lisa leaned closer, her heart pounding, and Harlo met her halfway. Their lips met in a soft, tentative kiss, one that spoke of trust and the promise of something more.

When they pulled away, Lisa felt a mixture of exhilaration and fear.

"Was that okay?" Harlo asked, his voice low.

Lisa smiled, her cheeks warm. "Yeah. It was more than okay."

And for the first time in years, Lisa allowed herself to believe in the possibility of love again.

Chapter 12: Testing the Waters

The kiss lingered in Lisa's mind for days. It was a moment she replayed over and over, each time feeling a mix of excitement and fear. For the first time, she felt like she was standing on the edge of something real—something that could be good.

But life, as it often did, had its own plans.

The Rumors in Town
Willow Creek was a small town, and in small towns, news traveled fast. It wasn't long before whispers about Lisa and Harlo's budding relationship began to circulate.

"Did you hear? Lisa's been seeing that Harlo guy."
"Isn't she the woman who left her husband? What's her deal?"
"Harlo's nice, but doesn't she have a lot of... baggage?"

Lisa overheard snippets of conversations at the grocery store and felt the judgmental stares as she walked down the street. The gossip cut deeper than she wanted to admit.

That evening, Lisa confided in Maggie.

"They're talking about me like I'm some sort of charity case," Lisa said, her voice thick with frustration.

Maggie, ever the voice of reason, handed Lisa a steaming cup of tea. "People are always going to talk, Lisa. You can't control that."

"I know," Lisa said, sighing. "But it feels like they're questioning whether I even deserve to be happy."

Maggie leaned forward, her eyes kind but firm. "You don't need anyone else's approval. You've worked hard to rebuild your life, and you've earned every bit of joy that comes your way. Don't let a few busybodies take that from you."

Lisa nodded, though her resolve felt shaky.

Marcus's Return

A week later, Marcus showed up again. This time, it wasn't a chance encounter at the diner—it was deliberate. He came to Lisa's house, his car pulling into the driveway just as Harlo was leaving.

Lisa's stomach churned as she watched Marcus step out of the car, his expression smug and calculating.

"Well, well," Marcus said, his eyes flicking between Lisa and Harlo. "Didn't take you long to move on, did it?"

"That's none of your business," Lisa said, her voice tight.

Harlo stood beside her, his presence a steadying force. "You should leave," Harlo said calmly, though there was a quiet strength in his tone.

Marcus scoffed. "I'm not here to cause trouble. I just wanted to see my kids."

"They're adults now," Lisa said. "If they want to see you, that's up to them. But you don't get to come here uninvited."

Marcus's eyes narrowed. "You think you can just erase me from their lives? From your life?"

"No one's erasing you," Harlo said, stepping forward. "But Lisa has a right to set boundaries. Respect them."

For a moment, Marcus looked like he might argue, but then he smirked. "You've got quite the guard dog, Lisa. Let's hope he sticks around."

With that, Marcus got back in his car and drove off, leaving a tense silence in his wake.

The Aftermath

Inside, Lisa paced the living room, her emotions swirling. "I can't believe he had the nerve to come here," she said.

Harlo watched her carefully. "Are you okay?"

"I don't know," she admitted, sinking onto the couch. "I thought I was past all of this, but he just... he knows how to get under my skin."

Harlo sat beside her, his presence calm and grounding. "It's normal to feel shaken. But you handled it well."

Lisa looked at him, her eyes searching his. "You don't think I'm... too much to deal with?"

Harlo frowned. "Lisa, don't ever think that. You're not too much. Marcus is the one who can't let go. That's on him, not you."

Her chest tightened, but this time it wasn't fear—it was gratitude.

A Test of Trust

That weekend, Lisa hesitated when Harlo invited her to a community picnic.

"I'm not sure it's a good idea," she said. "People are already talking."

"Let them talk," Harlo said gently. "What they think doesn't matter. What matters is how you feel."

Lisa thought about it for a long moment, then nodded. "Okay. Let's go."

At the picnic, Lisa felt the weight of the town's eyes on her. She heard the whispers and saw the sideways glances.

But then she looked at Harlo, who was helping Kyle set up a horseshoe game, and Mia, who was laughing with Maggie's daughter.

For the first time, Lisa realized she didn't need the approval of anyone else. Her happiness wasn't up for debate.

An Argument and a Revelation
That evening, after the picnic, Lisa and Harlo sat on her porch.

"I saw the way people were looking at me," Lisa said. "And for a moment, I almost let it ruin the day."

"But you didn't," Harlo said.

"No," Lisa said, smiling faintly. "I didn't."

Harlo hesitated, then said, "Lisa, I need you to know something. I'm in this—for real. But if you're not ready, if this is too much, I'll understand."

Lisa's heart ached at the vulnerability in his voice.

"I'm scared," she admitted. "But I'm also tired of being scared. I don't want to let fear control my life anymore."

Harlo reached for her hand, his grip warm and steady. "Then we'll face it together. One step at a time."

For the first time, Lisa felt like she wasn't just surviving—she was living. And with Harlo by her side, she knew she could face whatever challenges came their way.

Chapter 13: Embracing the Light

The days that followed felt different for Lisa. There was a sense of clarity she hadn't experienced in years, as if she'd finally stepped out from the shadows of her past. The whispers and judgments of others faded into the background, no longer weighing her down.

More importantly, Lisa had begun to embrace the idea that she deserved happiness—not just for her children, but for herself.

A Morning of Joy
One crisp morning, Lisa woke early, the house still quiet. She brewed a pot of coffee and sat by the window, watching the golden sunlight spill across her garden.

The birdhouse Harlo had built was now home to a pair of sparrows, their soft chirping filling the air. Lisa smiled, feeling a warmth in her chest that wasn't tinged with fear or doubt.

When Harlo arrived later that morning, carrying a basket of freshly baked muffins, Lisa greeted him with a smile that reached her eyes.

"Good morning," he said, his grin widening when he saw her.

"It is," Lisa replied, meaning it.

A Day at the Beach
That weekend, Harlo suggested a trip to the beach. Lisa hesitated at first—she hadn't been to the ocean in years, and the thought of exposing herself in any vulnerable way still felt daunting.

But then Mia and Kyle chimed in, excited at the idea, and Lisa found herself saying yes.

The drive to the coast was filled with laughter and music. Harlo and Kyle joked about who would catch the biggest crab, while Mia peppered her mother with questions about seashells and tide pools.

When they arrived, Lisa stood for a moment, letting the salty breeze wash over her. The sound of waves crashing against the shore was soothing, almost meditative.

Harlo set up a small picnic area while Lisa and Mia walked along the shoreline, their bare feet sinking into the cool, wet sand.

"You seem happy," Mia said, glancing up at her mother.

Lisa paused, surprised by her daughter's observation. "I think I am," she admitted.

Mia smiled. "I like Harlo. He makes you smile."

Lisa laughed softly. "He does, doesn't he?"

A Moment of Connection
As the sun began to set, Lisa found herself sitting beside Harlo on a large driftwood log. The kids were further down the beach, laughing as they tried to build a sandcastle before the tide claimed it.

Lisa glanced at Harlo, who was watching the horizon with a thoughtful expression.

"What are you thinking about?" she asked.

He turned to her, his eyes warm. "How lucky I am to be here with you."

Lisa felt her cheeks flush. "I don't know how you do it," she said.

"Do what?"

"Stay so patient. So steady."

Harlo shrugged. "You're worth it, Lisa. And I know this hasn't been easy for you. But seeing you like this—happy, relaxed—it makes it all worth it."

Lisa reached over, hesitating for only a moment before taking his hand. "Thank you," she said softly.

"For what?"

"For showing me that it's okay to trust again."

Harlo squeezed her hand gently. "You did that yourself, Lisa. I just gave you the space to see it."

A Night of Reflection
That night, after the kids were asleep and Harlo had gone home, Lisa sat on her porch, staring up at the stars.

Her mind drifted back to the years she'd spent in fear and doubt, trapped in a cycle she thought she'd never escape. The person she was now felt like a stranger to that version of herself—a stranger she was proud to know.

For the first time in years, Lisa felt truly free.

A New Beginning
In the weeks that followed, Lisa continued to embrace this new phase of her life. She took up painting, something she'd loved as a teenager but had abandoned in her marriage. She joined a book club, laughing and sharing stories with a group of women who quickly became friends.

And with Harlo, she let herself dream. They talked about everything—about their fears and hopes, their favorite childhood memories, and the futures they imagined.

One evening, as they sat together on the porch, Harlo turned to her with a smile.

"Do you ever think about what's next?" he asked.

Lisa tilted her head. "What do you mean?"

"For us," Harlo said, his tone light but sincere.

Lisa felt a flicker of fear but pushed it aside. "I do," she admitted. "And for the first time, it doesn't scare me."

Harlo smiled, reaching for her hand. "Good. Because I think we have something worth holding onto."

Lisa nodded, her heart swelling with a mix of excitement and peace.

"I think so too," she said.

And for the first time in her life, Lisa felt ready—not just for love, but for all the possibilities that lay ahead.

Chapter 14: A Significant Step Forward

Lisa stood in front of her bedroom mirror, smoothing out the folds of her deep blue dress. It wasn't extravagant, but the way it hugged her figure and brought out her skin's warm undertones made her feel beautiful—something she hadn't felt in years.

Tonight was special. Harlo had invited her to a dinner party at his friend's house. It wasn't just any gathering; these were people who mattered to him, people he trusted. It was his way of taking their relationship to the next level.

But as Lisa looked at herself, doubt began to creep in.

"Mom, you look amazing," Mia said, standing in the doorway.

Lisa turned to see her daughter beaming at her. "You think so?"

"Definitely. Harlo's going to love it."

Lisa smiled, though the nervous flutter in her stomach remained.

The Dinner Party

The drive to the dinner party was filled with quiet conversation. Harlo sensed Lisa's nervousness and kept his tone light, telling stories about his quirky friend Dave, who was hosting.

When they arrived, Lisa was greeted warmly. Dave was a jovial man with a booming laugh, and his wife, Sheila, immediately took Lisa under her wing, introducing her to the other guests.

Lisa felt out of place at first. The other women seemed confident and carefree, discussing vacations, work, and their children's achievements. But as the evening wore on, she found herself laughing at Dave's jokes and sharing stories of her own.

Harlo stayed close but gave her space to find her footing. He'd glance at her occasionally, his eyes filled with quiet pride.

When dinner was served, Lisa found herself seated between Sheila and Harlo. The conversation flowed easily, and Lisa felt a sense of belonging she hadn't experienced in a long time.

A Test of Confidence

As the night went on, one of the guests, a sharp-tongued woman named Valerie, turned the conversation toward Lisa.

"So, how long have you and Harlo been... seeing each other?" Valerie asked, her tone polite but pointed.

Lisa hesitated, feeling the weight of the room's attention.

"Not too long," Lisa replied carefully. "But it's been wonderful so far."

Valerie raised an eyebrow. "You're brave, stepping into a relationship again after everything you've been through. It must be... challenging."

The comment stung, but before Lisa could respond, Harlo stepped in.

"It's not about bravery," Harlo said firmly. "It's about finding someone who makes you want to move forward, no matter what you've been through. Lisa does that for me."

The room fell silent for a moment, and then Sheila chimed in with a warm smile. "That's beautifully said, Harlo. And Lisa, you're clearly a remarkable woman."

Lisa felt her cheeks flush, but the knot in her chest loosened.

A Private Moment
Later, as the party wound down and guests began to leave, Harlo and Lisa found themselves alone on the back patio. The cool night air was refreshing, and the sound of crickets filled the silence.

"You handled Valerie like a pro," Harlo said, leaning against the railing.

Lisa chuckled. "I almost let her get to me."

"But you didn't," Harlo said, his voice warm. "I'm proud of you, Lisa."

Lisa looked at him, her heart swelling. "I don't know if I could've done this without you."

"You could've," Harlo said. "But I'm glad I get to be here with you."

He reached out, tucking a strand of hair behind her ear. The gesture was so gentle, so intimate, that Lisa felt her breath catch.

"I've been thinking," Harlo said, his tone careful but sincere.

"About what?"

"About us," he said. "About what this means. I want you to know that I'm all in, Lisa. Whatever this becomes, I'm here for it."

Lisa felt a rush of emotions—fear, hope, love. She took a deep breath, meeting his gaze.

"I'm scared," she admitted. "But I want this too. I want... us."

Harlo smiled, and in that moment, Lisa felt a sense of peace she hadn't known was possible.

A New Chapter
When they returned home that night, Lisa felt different—lighter. She knew there would still be challenges, still moments of doubt and fear, but for the first time, she felt ready to face them.

The next morning, as she sat on the porch sipping her coffee, Harlo arrived with his usual easy smile.

"Good morning," he said, holding up a box of pastries.

"Good morning," Lisa replied, her own smile coming easily.

And as they sat together, watching the sun rise over Willow Creek, Lisa knew she was stepping into a new chapter of her life—one filled with love, hope, and the promise of something beautiful.

Chapter 15: Blending Lives

Blending their lives together wasn't something Lisa or Harlo had rushed into. Both had lived full, complicated lives before meeting, and merging those histories was bound to come with challenges. But they agreed to take things one step at a time.

Testing the Waters

The first real test came one Saturday afternoon when Harlo invited Lisa and her kids over for dinner at his house. Lisa had been to Harlo's home before, but this time felt different. It was the first time she would see her children interact with him in a space that was entirely his.

Harlo's home was warm and inviting, with an eclectic mix of furniture that reflected his personality: sturdy and unpretentious, but with bursts of charm—like the mismatched cushions on his couch and the vibrant paintings on the walls.

Kyle was the first to break the ice. "So, Harlo," he said as they sat down to eat, "do you cook all this yourself, or did you bribe someone?"

Harlo chuckled. "I did it myself. But don't ask me to bake—I'd burn water if I tried."

Kyle laughed, and Lisa felt a wave of relief wash over her.

Mia, however, was quieter, picking at her food. Lisa noticed but decided not to push her.

After dinner, Harlo suggested a game of cards, and the evening ended with everyone laughing over Kyle's failed attempts to bluff. Even Mia seemed to relax by the end of the night.

Navigating Space

As their relationship deepened, Harlo began spending more time at Lisa's house. While it felt natural for them, adjusting to his presence was an entirely new experience for Lisa's kids.

One evening, as Lisa and Harlo cooked dinner together, Mia walked into the kitchen.

"Mom," she said, crossing her arms, "do you really think this is a good idea?"

Lisa turned from the stove, her brow furrowing. "What do you mean?"

"With Harlo," Mia said, glancing at him. "It's just... weird seeing someone else here. It's like Dad all over again."

Lisa froze, her stomach knotting. She had worked so hard to create a safe, stable environment for her kids, and the last thing she wanted was to disrupt that.

Harlo, sensing the tension, stepped in. "Mia," he said gently, "I'm not here to take your dad's place. I know how important he is to you, no matter what's happened. I just want to be someone who supports your mom and respects this family."

Mia hesitated, her expression softening slightly. "It's just... gonna take some time."

"That's okay," Lisa said, her voice steady. "We'll take all the time we need."

Harlo's Own Challenges

Harlo had his own hurdles to overcome. His friends and family had questions about Lisa and her past, and while most were supportive, a few weren't shy about voicing their concerns.

"She's been through a lot, Harlo," his sister Ruth said one evening over the phone. "Are you sure you're ready for all of that?"

"I'm not afraid of her past, Ruth," Harlo replied. "I'm more interested in her future—and I want to be part of it."

Ruth sighed. "Just be careful, okay? You've been hurt before too."

"I will," Harlo promised. But his resolve never wavered.

Finding Balance

Over time, Lisa and Harlo began finding a rhythm. They took turns hosting dinners, spent lazy Sundays reading on the porch, and navigated the intricacies of their schedules and responsibilities.

One night, as they sat together planning a weekend trip, Lisa looked at Harlo and smiled.

"This is harder than I thought it would be," she admitted. "But it's also... good. Really good."

Harlo reached for her hand. "Anything worth having takes work. But I think we're doing okay."

Lisa nodded, feeling a quiet confidence she hadn't known before.

A New Milestone

The first real breakthrough came when Mia asked Harlo for help with her car.

"Mom said you're good with engines," Mia said, her tone cautious but hopeful.

"I know a thing or two," Harlo replied with a grin. "Let's take a look."

As Lisa watched from the window, she saw Mia laughing at something Harlo said, her posture more relaxed than it had been in weeks.

Later that evening, Mia surprised Lisa by saying, "I think Harlo's... okay. He's not trying too hard, you know? He just... is."

Lisa smiled, her heart swelling with gratitude.

An Unspoken Agreement
One evening, as they sat together on the couch, Lisa turned to Harlo.

"Do you ever feel like we're taking on too much?" she asked.

Harlo considered her question, then shook his head. "No. It's not always easy, but nothing worth having ever is. And I think we're worth it, Lisa."

Lisa leaned into him, resting her head on his shoulder.

"I think so too," she said softly.

And in that moment, she realized they weren't just blending their lives—they were building something entirely new.

Chapter 16: Taking the Leap

The idea had been floating in the air for weeks, unspoken but ever-present. Lisa and Harlo had reached a point where their time together was less about dating and more about blending their everyday lives. Harlo was at Lisa's house so often he had a designated coffee mug, and Lisa found herself leaving a scarf or a book at Harlo's place without realizing it.

But moving in together—making that leap—wasn't just about convenience. It was about trust, commitment, and the weight of their histories.

The First Conversation
One Sunday afternoon, as they sat on Harlo's porch enjoying the breeze, he broached the subject.

"You know," Harlo began, his voice light but deliberate, "I feel like I spend more time at your place than my own these days."

Lisa chuckled. "You do. Not that I mind."

"I don't either," Harlo said, turning to look at her. "But it got me thinking—what if we didn't have to split our time between two houses?"

Lisa froze, her coffee cup halfway to her lips. The idea was thrilling but also terrifying.

"Are you saying... you want to move in together?" she asked cautiously.

Harlo nodded, his expression earnest. "I do. But only if you're ready. There's no rush, Lisa. I just want you to think about it."

Lisa nodded slowly, her mind racing.

Weighing the Decision
That night, after Harlo had gone home, Lisa found herself sitting on her bed, staring at the framed photo of her kids on her nightstand. She thought about everything she'd built since leaving her ex—the sanctuary she'd created in her home, the routines that brought her comfort.

But then she thought about Harlo—the way he made her laugh, the way he respected her space and her past. She thought about the quiet joy she felt when they were together.

Still, doubt lingered. Would moving in together disrupt the delicate balance she'd worked so hard to achieve?

A Family Discussion
The next evening, Lisa sat down with Kyle and Mia. She hadn't expected to involve them in the decision, but she realized how important their input was.

"So," Lisa began, fiddling with the edge of her sweater, "Harlo and I have been talking about something... big."

Mia raised an eyebrow. "Big how?"

Lisa took a deep breath. "He suggested we consider moving in together."

Kyle leaned back in his chair, his expression thoughtful. "Wow. That's... a big step."

"It is," Lisa agreed. "And I wanted to know how you both feel about it. I know this would be a big change for all of us."

Mia was quiet for a moment, then said, "I like Harlo, Mom. He's a good guy. But are you sure you're ready? After everything?"

Lisa nodded. "That's what I'm trying to figure out. But I don't want to make this decision without considering you two."

Kyle shrugged. "Harlo's already around a lot, and I don't mind. If you think it's the right thing to do, I'm okay with it."

Mia nodded slowly. "Me too. As long as you're happy, Mom."

Lisa felt a surge of gratitude and pride. "Thank you," she said, her voice thick with emotion.

Taking the Leap
Two weeks later, Lisa and Harlo stood in her living room, surrounded by boxes.

"This feels surreal," Lisa admitted, holding a framed photo of her kids.

Harlo smiled. "Good surreal or bad surreal?"

"Good," Lisa said, setting the frame on the mantel. "But also scary."

Harlo stepped closer, taking her hands in his. "We'll figure it out together. One step at a time."

Lisa nodded, her heart steadying at his touch.

The First Night
That evening, after the kids had gone to bed and the house was quiet, Lisa and Harlo sat on the couch, the faint glow of the TV illuminating the room.

"How does it feel?" Harlo asked, his arm draped around her shoulders.

"Different," Lisa admitted. "But good. Really good."

Harlo smiled, pressing a kiss to her temple. "Here's to our new chapter."

Lisa leaned into him, feeling a warmth she hadn't known in years. For the first time, she wasn't just surviving—she was thriving.

Chapter 17: The Realities of Togetherness

The first few weeks of living together felt like a honeymoon phase. Lisa and Harlo fell into easy routines—cooking dinner side by side, taking walks through the neighborhood, and sharing quiet mornings over coffee. But as the days turned into weeks, the realities of merging two lives began to surface.

Small Adjustments
Lisa was a stickler for organization, and her home reflected that. Every book, every plate, every throw pillow had its place. Harlo, on the other hand, was more relaxed. He left coffee mugs on counters, forgot to close cabinet doors, and once folded the towels "wrong."

One evening, as Lisa straightened the living room for the third time that day, she caught herself muttering under her breath.

"Harlo, can we talk?" she said, turning to him as he watched TV.

He muted the show and sat up. "What's up?"

Lisa hesitated, not wanting to sound critical. "It's just... I'm used to things being a certain way. Like the towels. They go in the closet with the folded edges facing out."

Harlo chuckled, but his expression was kind. "I had no idea towel folding was such an art form."

"It's not just the towels," Lisa said, trying not to laugh. "It's a lot of little things. I guess I'm just... adjusting."

Harlo nodded. "I get it. And I'll try to be more mindful. But you might have to cut me some slack—I've been living solo for years."

Lisa smiled, feeling a weight lift. "Fair enough. I'll try to loosen up too."

Blending Traditions
One Saturday, Harlo announced that he wanted to cook dinner—a dish his mother used to make. Lisa watched as he pulled out ingredients she'd never used before, the kitchen soon filled with the rich, spicy aroma of gumbo.

When the meal was ready, Lisa and her kids sat down to eat, their plates piled high.

"This is amazing," Kyle said after his first bite.

"It's really good," Lisa agreed, though the heat of the spices made her eyes water.

Mia grinned. "Mom's not used to food this spicy."

Lisa laughed, reaching for her water. "I'll get there."

Later, as they cleaned up, Lisa said, "I love that you're sharing this with us. It's nice to try something new."

Harlo smiled. "I think that's what this is all about—bringing our worlds together."

A Misunderstanding
One evening, Harlo came home later than expected, his mood tense. Lisa noticed immediately but decided to give him space.

As the evening wore on, the tension grew palpable. Finally, Lisa couldn't take it anymore.

"Is something wrong?" she asked, her voice careful.

Harlo sighed, rubbing his face. "It's nothing."

"It doesn't feel like nothing," Lisa said, sitting beside him. "Talk to me."

Harlo hesitated before saying, "Work's been stressful. And I guess... I'm still getting used to this. Being accountable to someone else again."

Lisa felt a pang of guilt. "I didn't mean to make you feel pressured."

"You didn't," Harlo said quickly. "This is on me. I've been on my own for so long, and sometimes I forget how to... share my life."

Lisa took his hand. "We're both learning, Harlo. And it's okay to have hard days. Just don't shut me out, okay?"

Harlo nodded, his expression softening. "Deal."

Finding Their Rhythm
As time went on, Lisa and Harlo found a balance. They learned to navigate each other's quirks—Lisa learned to let go of the little things, and Harlo made an effort to meet her halfway.

One evening, as they sat on the porch watching the sunset, Harlo said, "You know, I think we're doing pretty good at this whole living-together thing."

Lisa laughed. "We're not bad for a couple of stubborn old souls."

Harlo grinned. "Speak for yourself. I'm practically a saint."

Lisa swatted his arm, and they both laughed, the sound carrying into the evening air.

A Shared Future
As they settled into their new life, Lisa began to feel something she hadn't felt in years—peace. For the first time, she wasn't looking over her shoulder or bracing for the next storm.

And as she sat beside Harlo, watching the stars blink into the night sky, she realized she wasn't just building a life with him—she was building a home.

Chapter 18: A Storm from the Outside

Life had settled into a comfortable rhythm for Lisa and Harlo, but as they grew closer, the universe seemed determined to test their resolve. The storm came in the form of Lisa's ex-husband, Charles, who had been little more than a distant, painful memory.

Until he showed up.

An Unexpected Encounter

Lisa was walking out of the grocery store one crisp Saturday morning, arms full of bags, when she saw him. Charles stood by his car, his lean frame as familiar as the tightness that gripped her chest.

"Lisa," he called out, a smile playing on his lips as if the years hadn't passed, as if he hadn't left scars she was still learning to heal.

Lisa froze, her heart pounding. "Charles," she said, her voice steady despite the storm brewing inside her.

"Been a while," he said casually, stepping closer.

"Not long enough," she muttered under her breath.

He caught her tone but ignored it. "I've been meaning to reach out. I wanted to see how you've been."

"I'm fine," Lisa said curtly, shifting the bags in her arms.

"I heard about you and Harlo," Charles continued, his tone laced with something she couldn't quite place—jealousy, perhaps, or curiosity. "Small town and all."

Lisa stiffened. "What do you want, Charles?"

"Just to talk," he said, his hands up in mock surrender. "Maybe catch up. For old times' sake."

"There's nothing to catch up on," Lisa said, her voice cold. "Leave me alone."

She turned and walked away, her hands trembling as she loaded her groceries into the car.

The Aftermath
When Lisa got home, Harlo immediately noticed her unease.

"You okay?" he asked, setting down his coffee.

Lisa hesitated before nodding. "I ran into Charles."

Harlo's expression darkened. "What did he want?"

"To talk," Lisa said, sinking onto the couch. "I told him to leave me alone, but it rattled me."

Harlo reached for her hand. "You don't have to deal with him alone, Lisa. If he comes back, we'll handle it together."

His words comforted her, but the encounter left a lingering unease that neither could shake.

An Unwelcome Visitor
A week later, Charles showed up at Lisa's house.

Harlo was outside working on the car when Charles pulled into the driveway.

"Can I help you?" Harlo said, standing tall as Charles stepped out of the car.

"I'm here to see Lisa," Charles said, his tone dismissive.

Harlo crossed his arms. "She doesn't want to see you."

Charles smirked. "And who are you to decide that?"

"I'm the man who cares about her," Harlo said firmly. "And I'm not going to let you disrupt her life."

Lisa appeared at the door then, her heart racing.

"Charles, I told you to leave me alone," she said, her voice sharp.

"I just want to talk," Charles said, his expression softening. "I've changed, Lisa. I want to make amends."

Lisa hesitated, her mind flashing back to all the times he'd said those same words before.

"I don't believe you," she said finally. "And even if I did, I've moved on. You need to do the same."

Charles's face hardened, but he said nothing as he turned and got into his car.

Strength in Unity
That night, as Lisa and Harlo sat on the couch, she leaned into him, her head resting on his chest.

"Thank you for standing up for me," she said softly.

"You don't have to thank me for that," Harlo replied. "We're a team, Lisa. Whatever comes our way, we'll face it together."

Lisa smiled, feeling a deep sense of gratitude. For years, she had faced her battles alone, but now she had someone by her side.

And for the first time in a long time, she felt truly safe.

Chapter 19: A Milestone Worth Celebrating

The air buzzed with quiet excitement as Lisa set the dining room table, the warm scent of roasted chicken and herbs wafting from the kitchen. Tonight wasn't just any dinner; it marked one year since Harlo had moved in with her—a milestone that Lisa felt was worth celebrating.

For years, she had shied away from acknowledging anniversaries or special moments. They reminded her too much of the empty promises of her past. But with Harlo, everything felt different. This time, she wanted to celebrate not just their relationship but her own growth.

Preparing for the Evening

"Do you need help with anything?" Harlo called from the living room, where he was attempting to tie a new bowtie—something Lisa had suggested for the occasion.

"You could check on the dessert," Lisa replied, smiling as she adjusted the candles on the table.

A moment later, Harlo appeared in the kitchen, his tie slightly askew but his grin charming as ever. "How do I look?"

Lisa turned, her eyes scanning him appreciatively. "Like someone I'm very lucky to have in my life."

He stepped closer, wrapping his arms around her waist. "The feeling's mutual."

Lisa felt the familiar flutter in her chest, a warmth that still caught her off guard.

An Unexpected Toast

The evening began with laughter as Lisa's children, Kyle and Mia, joined them for dinner. Though the kids were adults now, their presence made the house feel alive.

"You've done something amazing with this place, Mom," Mia said, raising her glass of sparkling cider. "It feels... full of love."

Lisa's throat tightened as she glanced at Harlo. "It's not just me. Harlo's been a big part of that."

"Well," Harlo said, clearing his throat, "since we're toasting, I'd like to say something."

He stood, holding his glass, his expression earnest. "This past year has been the best of my life. Lisa, you've shown me what love is supposed to feel like. And to Kyle and Mia—thank you for welcoming me into your family. I'm grateful every day to be here with all of you."

The table fell silent for a moment before Kyle spoke up, raising his glass. "To Harlo—and to Mom, for letting happiness back into her life."

The clink of glasses was followed by warm laughter and shared smiles.

A Quiet Moment Together

After the kids left and the house grew quiet, Lisa and Harlo sat on the porch, a blanket draped over their laps as they sipped the last of the cider.

"This was a good idea," Lisa said, leaning her head against Harlo's shoulder.

"I'm glad you thought so," Harlo replied, his arm wrapped securely around her.

For a while, they sat in comfortable silence, the stars twinkling overhead. Then Harlo broke the quiet.

"I've been thinking about something," he began, his tone serious.

Lisa glanced up at him. "What's on your mind?"

Harlo hesitated for a moment before taking her hand. "I know we've talked about taking things slow, and I don't want to rush anything. But... I can't imagine my life without you. I think I'd like to make this official someday—when you're ready."

Lisa's heart raced, but not with fear. For the first time, the idea of a future with someone didn't feel suffocating—it felt hopeful.

"Someday," she said softly, squeezing his hand. "When we're both ready."

Harlo smiled, his eyes warm. "I can live with that."

A New Chapter Begins
As they sat together under the stars, Lisa felt something shift inside her. She wasn't just surviving anymore—she was living, growing, and embracing a future filled with possibilities.

For the first time, she truly believed that happiness wasn't fleeting—it was something she could build, nurture, and share.

And with Harlo by her side, she knew that whatever came next, they would face it together.

Chapter 20: Through the Storm

The rain came suddenly, battering against the windows with a force that seemed almost vengeful. Lisa sat at the kitchen table, a cup of tea growing cold in her hands, her eyes flickering to the darkened sky outside.

"I haven't seen a storm like this in years," Harlo said, walking in from the living room and setting his phone on the counter. "Looks like the whole town's bracing for it."

Lisa nodded, her mind elsewhere. She couldn't shake the sense of unease that had settled over her since the power had flickered earlier.

"Everything okay?" Harlo asked, sitting beside her.

"I'm fine," Lisa replied, forcing a smile. "Just... storms bring back memories."

Harlo placed a reassuring hand over hers, his warmth grounding her. "Well, if it helps, I'm here. We'll ride it out together."

The Power Goes Out

As if on cue, the lights flickered again before plunging the house into darkness.

"Great," Lisa muttered, standing to grab the flashlight she kept in a kitchen drawer.

Harlo chuckled. "Nothing like a little adventure."

"Adventure?" Lisa shot him a look. "More like a headache."

Harlo followed her with a flashlight of his own, its beam casting long shadows across the walls. "Come on, it's not so bad. Let's find the candles and make the best of it."

Within minutes, the house was aglow with the soft, flickering light of candles. The storm raged outside, but inside, a strange calm began to settle.

An Unlikely Emergency

Just as they started to relax, a frantic knock came at the door. Lisa and Harlo exchanged a look before Harlo moved to answer it.

A young woman stood on the porch, drenched from head to toe, clutching a small dog in her arms.

"Please," she said, her voice trembling. "My car broke down, and I didn't know where else to go."

Lisa quickly stepped forward, ushering her inside. "Come in before you catch your death. What's your name?"

"Emily," the woman replied, her teeth chattering.

Harlo grabbed a towel while Lisa guided Emily to the couch. The dog—a tiny terrier—whimpered in her arms, shivering as much as its owner.

"Where were you headed?" Harlo asked, handing her the towel.

"I was driving to my sister's," Emily explained. "But the storm was too much, and my car just stopped."

"Well, you're safe here," Lisa said firmly. "Let's get you warmed up."

Opening Their Home
Over the next few hours, Lisa and Harlo worked to make Emily comfortable. Lisa prepared tea and a light meal while Harlo checked the dog for injuries, his large hands surprisingly gentle as he wrapped the pup in a warm blanket.

"Thank you," Emily said, her voice thick with emotion. "I didn't know what I was going to do."

"You don't need to thank us," Harlo said with a smile. "We're just glad you found us."

As the storm continued to howl outside, the three of them settled in the living room. Emily shared bits of her story—how she'd been traveling to escape an unhealthy situation, much like Lisa had years ago.

Lisa listened intently, her heart aching for the young woman. "You're stronger than you realize," she told Emily, her voice steady. "Getting out is the hardest part, but it's the first step toward something better."

A Moment of Reflection
Later that night, after Emily had fallen asleep in the guest room, Lisa and Harlo sat on the couch, the candlelight casting soft shadows across their faces.

"You handled that beautifully," Harlo said, his voice low.

Lisa shook her head. "I just did what anyone would do."

"No," Harlo said, taking her hand. "You did what someone who understands does. You gave her what you never had—kindness, safety, hope."

Lisa felt tears prick at the corners of her eyes. "I guess I never thought about it like that."

Harlo leaned in, pressing a kiss to her forehead. "It's one of the things I love most about you—your heart."

Lisa smiled, her chest swelling with a mix of gratitude and love. For so long, she had doubted her own strength, but moments like this reminded her just how far she had come.

A Bond Forged in the Storm
By the time the storm passed, the house was quiet, save for the soft snores of the dog curled up in a blanket by the fire.

Lisa and Harlo sat together, their hands entwined as they watched the first rays of dawn peek through the clouds.

"You know," Lisa said softly, "this wasn't the evening I had in mind, but I wouldn't trade it for anything."

Harlo squeezed her hand. "Me neither. Sometimes it takes a storm to remind us what really matters."

As they sat together, Lisa felt a deep sense of peace. She and Harlo weren't just partners—they were a team, ready to face whatever life threw their way.

Chapter 21: The Ripple Effect

The morning after the storm, the house was filled with a quiet sense of relief. The rain had stopped, the winds had calmed, and the first rays of sunlight peeked through the clouds. Emily sat at the kitchen table with Lisa, cradling a steaming cup of coffee in her hands while Harlo busied himself in the backyard, clearing debris.

For the first time in what felt like forever, Emily looked at ease. The shadows of fear and exhaustion that had clouded her face the night before were beginning to lift.

"You really don't know how much this means to me," Emily said softly, breaking the silence.

Lisa gave her a warm smile. "I think I do. And you don't have to thank us. Everyone deserves a safe place to land."

A Shared Understanding
As they talked, Emily opened up further.

"I was in a relationship... not a good one," she admitted, her voice wavering. "I thought I could handle it, but last week, it got worse. That's when I decided to leave."

Lisa's chest tightened. Emily's story mirrored her own in so many ways, and it was almost like looking into a mirror of her past.

"You did the right thing," Lisa said, her tone firm but gentle. "It takes so much strength to walk away, but now you get to decide what's next for you."

Emily nodded, her eyes glistening with unshed tears. "How did you do it? How did you rebuild your life after leaving?"

Lisa took a deep breath, her mind flickering back to those first uncertain days after she left Charles. "One step at a time," she said. "I focused on the small victories—finding a safe place to stay, creating a routine, leaning on people who cared about me. And eventually, I realized that the past didn't have to define my future."

Harlo's Influence
When Harlo came back inside, his hands dusted with dirt, he grinned at the two women. "Yard's looking better already. Storm didn't leave too much damage."

Emily smiled shyly. "Thank you—for everything."

Harlo shrugged, his grin widening. "It's what we do around here. Besides, that little pup of yours has already won me over."

The terrier, now freshly washed and wagging its tail, barked as if in agreement, earning a laugh from everyone at the table.

"Do you have somewhere to go from here?" Harlo asked, his tone kind but concerned.

Emily hesitated. "I was heading to my sister's, but she's hours away. I don't even know if my car will make it."

Harlo glanced at Lisa, who nodded.

"You can stay here a few more days," Lisa offered. "Get some rest, figure out your next steps. We'll help however we can."

A Catalyst for Growth
Over the next few days, Emily became more than just a guest in Lisa and Harlo's home. She became a reminder of how far they had both come—and how much they had to give.

Lisa found herself reflecting on the journey that had brought her to this point. Seeing Emily take her first tentative steps toward independence and healing reignited a sense of purpose Lisa hadn't felt in years.

One afternoon, as they sat on the porch, Emily turned to Lisa.

"Do you think it's possible to trust someone again after... everything?"

Lisa thought about Harlo, about the walls she had built around her heart and the way he had patiently helped her take them down.

"I do," she said. "But it starts with trusting yourself first. When you learn to love yourself, the rest falls into place."

A Bond Strengthened
That evening, after Emily had gone to bed, Lisa and Harlo sat by the fire.

"She reminds me so much of myself," Lisa admitted, staring into the flickering flames.

Harlo reached for her hand. "And look at you now. You're living proof that things can get better."

Lisa smiled, leaning into him. "I wouldn't have made it this far without you."

Harlo kissed the top of her head. "Maybe. But you did the hard part—you chose to keep going."

As they sat together, Lisa felt a deep sense of pride—not just for how far she had come, but for the life she and Harlo were building. Emily's arrival had been unexpected, but it had reminded them both of the power of compassion and resilience.

And in helping Emily, they had found another way to grow closer.

Chapter 22: A Farewell and a New Beginning

The morning Emily planned to leave was bright and peaceful, as if the storm from days ago had never happened. Lisa stood in the kitchen, carefully packing a bag of snacks and water for Emily's trip, while Harlo worked on checking her car in the driveway.

Emily sat at the table with her little dog in her lap, a mix of gratitude and apprehension on her face.

"Are you sure the car's good to go?" she asked Harlo as he walked in, wiping his hands on a rag.

"Checked it twice," he assured her with a grin. "You'll make it to your sister's without a problem."

Lisa handed Emily the bag. "And this is for the road. It's not much, but it'll keep you and your pup fed until you get there."

Emily's eyes welled up. "I don't know how to thank you two. You didn't have to take me in, but you did. I'll never forget it."

"You don't need to thank us," Lisa said, her voice warm. "Just focus on moving forward. You've got this."

A Bittersweet Goodbye
When it was time for Emily to leave, Lisa and Harlo walked her to the car. The terrier barked excitedly from the passenger seat as Emily hugged Lisa tightly.

"You're stronger than you think," Lisa whispered, her voice steady.

Emily pulled back, her eyes shining. "So are you. Thank you for reminding me of that."

Harlo gave her a quick pat on the shoulder. "Take care of yourself, and don't be afraid to call if you need anything."

As Emily drove off, Lisa stood beside Harlo, watching until the car disappeared from view. For a long moment, they were quiet, both lost in their thoughts.

A Quiet Reflection
Later that evening, Lisa and Harlo sat on the back porch, sharing a bottle of wine as the sun dipped below the horizon.

"She's going to be okay," Lisa said, breaking the silence.

Harlo nodded. "Because she had someone like you to show her how."

Lisa turned to him, her expression thoughtful. "I never thought I'd be in a place where I could help someone else. For so long, I felt like I was just trying to survive."

Harlo reached for her hand, his grip firm and reassuring. "You didn't just survive, Lisa. You rebuilt yourself. And now, you're stronger for it."

She smiled, leaning her head against his shoulder. "It's funny—I thought Emily needed us, but I think I needed her just as much. She reminded me of where I came from, and how far I've come."

Harlo kissed the top of her head. "Life has a way of bringing people together at the right time."

A New Chapter Together
As the stars began to dot the sky, Lisa turned to Harlo with a newfound sense of clarity.

"I've been thinking," she said.

"About what?" he asked, his voice curious.

"About us," she replied. "I know I've been cautious—maybe even scared. But I'm ready to take the next step, whatever that looks like for us."

Harlo's eyes softened, his smile spreading slowly. "Lisa, there's no rush. We'll take it one day at a time, just like we always have."

She nodded, her heart swelling with love and gratitude. "One day at a time."

As they sat together, Lisa realized that her journey wasn't just about healing—it was about embracing the future with an open heart. And with Harlo by her side, she felt ready to face whatever came next.

Chapter 23: Building a Future Together

The idea started small, a passing comment one lazy Sunday morning as Lisa and Harlo sat on the porch sipping coffee. The birds chirped in the trees, the world was calm, and Lisa felt a rare sense of peace.

"You ever think about what's next for us?" Harlo asked, his voice casual but tinged with curiosity.

Lisa looked over at him, her brow furrowing slightly. "Next? Like... what do you mean?"

Harlo shrugged, a sheepish grin spreading across his face. "I mean... where do you see us in five years? Ten? Do you see us here, in this house, or somewhere else? Together, or...?"

Lisa tilted her head, studying his expression. She could see he was trying to tread carefully, but there was no mistaking the hope in his eyes.

"I've never been great at planning for the future," she admitted. "For so long, it felt like I couldn't even think beyond the next day."

Harlo reached over and took her hand, his touch warm and steady. "Well, maybe now's the time to start."

The Seed of an Idea
Over the next few weeks, the conversation lingered in Lisa's mind. Harlo didn't press her, but his words had planted a seed—a curiosity about what their future could look like if they built it together.

One evening, as they cooked dinner side by side, Lisa brought it up.

"Do you remember what you asked me a few weeks ago? About where I see us in the future?"

Harlo glanced at her, his face lighting up. "Of course. What about it?"

"I've been thinking," Lisa said slowly, setting down the cutting board. "I think I'd like to figure it out—together. Maybe even make some plans."

Harlo's smile widened, and he leaned against the counter. "I'm all ears."

Dreaming Together

They spent hours that night talking about their dreams. Harlo mentioned his desire to own a small woodworking shop, a place where he could craft furniture and teach others the trade.

Lisa surprised herself by admitting that she'd always wanted to open a community space—a warm, welcoming place where people could gather for classes, support groups, or just a cup of coffee and a conversation.

"I've never said that out loud before," Lisa confessed, her cheeks flushing.

"Why not?" Harlo asked, his tone gentle.

"I guess I didn't think it was possible," she admitted. "But now... I don't know. Maybe it is."

Harlo reached across the table, taking her hand. "Lisa, if anyone can make that happen, it's you. And you won't have to do it alone."

Taking the First Step

The next weekend, they took a drive to a nearby town where an old, run-down building had recently gone up for sale. Harlo had heard about it from a friend, and though they weren't ready to make any big decisions, they thought it might be worth a look.

The building was nothing fancy—faded brick, cracked windows, and overgrown weeds lining the walkway. But as Lisa stood in front of it, something stirred in her chest.

"What do you think?" Harlo asked, watching her carefully.

"I think..." Lisa paused, her eyes scanning the building. "I think it has potential."

Harlo grinned. "That's exactly what I thought."

They spent the afternoon exploring the space, imagining what it could become. Harlo pointed out where he could set up his workshop, while Lisa described how she'd furnish the community room with cozy chairs and bright artwork.

For the first time, Lisa allowed herself to dream—boldly, without fear of failure or judgment.

A Leap of Faith
That night, as they sat on the porch under a blanket of stars, Lisa turned to Harlo with a sense of determination.

"Let's do it," she said, her voice steady.

Harlo looked at her, his brow furrowing slightly. "Do what?"

"Let's buy the building," Lisa said. "Let's make it ours."

Harlo's face broke into a wide smile, and he pulled her into a tight hug. "Are you sure?"

"I've never been more sure," Lisa replied. "This is our chance to build something together—not just a space, but a life."

Harlo kissed her, his joy radiating through every fiber of his being. "Then let's do it."

The Beginning of Something New
In the weeks that followed, Lisa and Harlo began the process of turning their dream into reality. They met with realtors, drafted plans, and even started a savings plan to fund the renovations.

The journey was far from easy, but Lisa found herself energized by the challenge. For the first time in her life, she wasn't just surviving—she was creating, dreaming, and building a future filled with love, purpose, and hope.

And as she and Harlo stood hand in hand, watching the sun rise over the building that would soon become their shared legacy, Lisa knew they were exactly where they were meant to be.

Chapter 24: Building Dreams, Facing Challenges

The building felt like a blank canvas, waiting for Lisa and Harlo to bring it to life. Standing in the middle of the dusty floor with sunlight streaming through cracked windows, Lisa could already see flashes of what the space could become: vibrant walls filled with local art, warm chairs for people to gather, and shelves lined with books and supplies for workshops.

But with every beautiful vision came the reality: the building needed work—a lot of it.

The First Hurdles
"Plumbing's going to be a nightmare," Harlo said, crouching near an exposed pipe in what would one day be the kitchen.

Lisa sighed, leaning against the doorway. "And don't get me started on the roof. Did you see those leaks near the back room?"

Harlo stood and dusted off his hands. "We knew this wasn't going to be easy, Lisa. But we'll figure it out."

Their optimism was tested almost immediately. As they brought in contractors for estimates, the costs began to add up quickly. The budget they had meticulously planned for wasn't enough to cover half of what the building needed.

Lisa found herself lying awake at night, staring at the ceiling, wondering if they had made a mistake.

Tension in the Air
One evening, as they reviewed yet another estimate at the dining table, Lisa slammed her pen down in frustration.

"This isn't going to work," she said, her voice tight. "We can't afford all of this. What were we thinking?"

Harlo, who had been unusually quiet, looked up from the paperwork. "We were thinking that we wanted to create something meaningful," he said evenly. "And we still can. We just have to adjust."

"Adjust?" Lisa snapped. "Harlo, this isn't like fixing up a chair or a table. We're talking about thousands of dollars we don't have."

Harlo's jaw tightened, but he kept his voice calm. "I know it's overwhelming, but we can't give up now. We'll find a way."

The argument hung in the air, leaving a crack in their usually steady partnership.

Finding Strength Together
The next morning, Harlo surprised Lisa with two cups of coffee and a notebook.

"What's this?" she asked, eyeing him warily.

"A fresh start," he said, setting the notebook on the table. "I've been thinking. We can't do everything at once, but we can prioritize. Let's write down the absolute must-haves and focus on those first."

Lisa hesitated, then nodded. "Okay. Let's try it."

As they worked together, the tension began to fade. Lisa realized that Harlo wasn't just her partner in love—he was her partner in everything. His calm determination balanced her moments of doubt, and his unwavering belief in their vision reignited her own.

Rallying the Community

A week later, Harlo had an idea.

"Why don't we ask for help?" he suggested.

Lisa raised an eyebrow. "From who?"

"The community," Harlo said. "This isn't just for us—it's for everyone. Let's hold a fundraiser or a volunteer day. See who wants to pitch in."

Lisa hesitated, the thought of asking for help making her uneasy. But the more she considered it, the more it made sense.

Together, they organized a "Building Dreams Day," inviting neighbors and friends to come by the property to lend a hand or make donations toward the renovations.

A Day of Hope

On the morning of the event, Lisa's heart swelled as she watched people arrive. Some brought tools, others brought baked goods to sell, and a few even brought their children to help clean up the space.

"This is amazing," Lisa whispered to Harlo as she watched a group of volunteers clearing debris from the backyard.

"I told you," he said, grinning. "People want to be part of something good."

By the end of the day, they had raised enough money to cover the roof repairs and had a small team of volunteers committed to helping with future projects.

Rekindled Confidence

That night, as they sat in the nearly empty building, Lisa looked around at the progress they had made. The walls were still bare, and the floors were still scuffed, but the space already felt different—alive with possibility.

"I don't know how you do it," Lisa said, turning to Harlo.

"Do what?" he asked, smiling.

"Keep believing, even when things feel impossible."

Harlo took her hand. "Because I believe in us, Lisa. And I know we can handle whatever comes our way."

For the first time in weeks, Lisa felt a deep sense of calm. They still had a long road ahead, but with Harlo by her side, she knew they could navigate it together.

Chapter 25: The Grand Opening

The morning of the grand opening dawned bright and clear, a perfect California day. Lisa stood in the middle of the newly renovated space, taking in the results of months of hard work. The walls were painted in soft, welcoming hues, accented with art donated by local artists. The cozy furniture they had scoured secondhand stores for was arranged in inviting clusters. Shelves were stocked with books, supplies, and handmade crafts from the community.

"It's beautiful," Lisa murmured, her voice thick with emotion.

Harlo walked up behind her, sliding an arm around her waist. "It's more than beautiful—it's a dream come true."

Lisa smiled, leaning into him. "We did this together."

Harlo kissed her temple. "We sure did."

A Day to Celebrate
By mid-morning, people began arriving. Neighbors, friends, and even strangers who had heard about the project streamed through the doors, their faces lighting up as they explored the space.

Lisa found herself in a whirlwind of handshakes, hugs, and congratulations. Children ran excitedly to the art corner, while parents browsed the shelves and mingled with volunteers. Harlo stayed busy giving impromptu tours, proudly explaining the story behind every detail.

At one point, Lisa caught sight of a young woman sitting quietly in a corner, her head bowed over a cup of coffee. Something about her posture reminded Lisa of herself not too long ago—lost and searching.

Lisa approached her gently. "Hi, I'm Lisa. I'm so glad you're here."

The woman looked up, her eyes brimming with unshed tears. "I didn't think I'd stay," she admitted. "I'm not good at being around people right now."

Lisa sat down beside her. "I know that feeling," she said softly. "But you don't have to do this alone. That's what this place is for—to remind people they're not alone."

The woman nodded, a small smile tugging at her lips.

A Speech from the Heart
As the afternoon stretched on, Harlo insisted that Lisa give a speech. She protested, feeling nervous about standing in front of a crowd, but Harlo wouldn't take no for an answer.

"You're the heart of this place," he said, squeezing her hand. "People need to hear from you."

Taking a deep breath, Lisa stepped onto the small stage they had set up in the main room. The hum of conversation quieted as all eyes turned to her.

"Thank you all for being here," Lisa began, her voice steady despite the fluttering in her chest. "This space... it's more than just a building. It's a symbol of what's possible when people come together, when they support one another, and when they believe in second chances."

She paused, scanning the room. "There was a time when I didn't believe in much of anything—not myself, not the future, not love. But standing here today, I see how far I've come, and I see all of you. And I realize... none of this would've been possible without the kindness and generosity of this community. So, thank you—for believing in us, and for being part of this dream."

The crowd erupted into applause, and Lisa felt a swell of pride and gratitude unlike anything she'd ever experienced.

A Quiet Moment
As the evening wound down and the last guests trickled out, Lisa and Harlo sat on a couch in the middle of the space, surrounded by the echoes of laughter and conversation.

"We did it," Lisa said, her voice tinged with awe.

Harlo chuckled. "You're right. We really did."

Lisa turned to him, her eyes shining. "I couldn't have done this without you."

"And I wouldn't have wanted to do it without you," Harlo replied.

They sat in comfortable silence for a while, basking in the glow of their achievement.

The Beginning of Something New
That night, as they locked up the building and headed home, Lisa felt a profound sense of peace. The space they had created wasn't just a physical place—it was a testament to resilience, hope, and the power of love.

For the first time in her life, she felt truly at home—not just in the world, but within herself. And with Harlo by her side, she was ready to embrace whatever came next.

Chapter 26: A Promise of Forever

The weeks after the grand opening were a whirlwind of activity. The community space buzzed with life—art classes for children, support groups for single parents, and quiet corners where people found solace. Lisa threw herself into the work, her heart swelling with pride every time someone shared how the space had touched their lives.

Harlo was always by her side, steady and supportive. Whether he was fixing a stubborn chair leg or teaching a woodworking class, his presence grounded her.

One evening, after the last visitor had left and they were tidying up together, Harlo turned to Lisa with a thoughtful look.

"You know," he began, "I've been thinking about something."

Lisa glanced up, curious. "What's on your mind?"

Harlo hesitated for a moment, then set the broom aside. He took a deep breath and walked over to her, taking her hands in his.

"We've been through a lot together," he said, his voice steady but full of emotion. "We've built something beautiful here—not just this space, but our life. And I can't imagine any of it without you."

Lisa's heart began to race, her hands trembling slightly in his.

"Harlo..."

He smiled, reaching into his pocket and pulling out a small velvet box. Lisa's breath caught as he opened it to reveal a simple, elegant ring.

"I know you've been through a lot," Harlo continued. "And I know it hasn't been easy to let someone in. But I love you, Lisa. With everything I have. And I want to spend the rest of my life with you. Will you marry me?"

A Moment of Silence
Lisa stared at the ring, her emotions swirling—joy, fear, love, uncertainty—all at once.

"Harlo, I..." she began, her voice faltering.

Harlo didn't let go of her hands. "It's okay," he said softly. "You don't have to answer right now. I just needed you to know how I feel."

Lisa blinked back tears, overwhelmed by his patience and understanding. She had never felt this kind of love before—steady, unwavering, free of pressure.

"I need some time," she admitted, her voice barely above a whisper.

Harlo nodded, his expression gentle. "Take all the time you need."

Reflection
That night, Lisa lay awake in bed, the ring box sitting on her nightstand. She stared at it, memories flooding her mind—her past pain, her journey of healing, and the love she had found with Harlo.

She thought about the way he had stood by her, never pushing, always supporting. The way he believed in her when she couldn't believe in herself.

And she realized something: she wasn't afraid of Harlo or his love. She was afraid of losing herself again, of repeating the mistakes of her past. But deep down, she knew that Harlo was different. Their love was different.

A Decision

The next morning, Lisa woke with a sense of clarity. She dressed carefully, slipping the ring box into her bag, and made her way to the community space where Harlo was already working.

When she walked in, he looked up from his project, a hopeful but cautious smile on his face.

"Hey," he said. "Everything okay?"

Lisa nodded, walking over to him. She took a deep breath, pulling the ring box from her bag and placing it in his hands.

"Harlo," she began, her voice steady. "I've been scared. Not of you, but of what it means to open myself up like this. But if there's one thing I've learned from you, it's that love doesn't have to hurt. It can heal. And I want to keep healing—with you."

She smiled, tears welling in her eyes. "Yes, Harlo. I'll marry you."

A New Beginning

Harlo's face broke into a radiant smile, and he pulled her into his arms, holding her tightly.

"You've just made me the happiest man alive," he whispered, his voice thick with emotion.

As he slipped the ring onto her finger, Lisa felt a sense of peace and joy she had never known before. This wasn't just a new chapter in her life—it was the beginning of a love story she could truly believe in.

Chapter 27: Planning the Promise

The days after Harlo's proposal were filled with a new sense of joy and anticipation. For the first time in years, Lisa felt as though she was walking on solid ground. She couldn't stop glancing at the ring on her finger, the delicate band glinting like a quiet promise of a beautiful future.

Harlo was just as thrilled, though his excitement was quieter, more measured. He wanted the wedding to be perfect, but more than that, he wanted Lisa to feel fully in control of the process.

The First Conversations
One evening, as they sat together on the couch, Harlo broached the topic.

"So, have you thought about what kind of wedding you want?" he asked, his hand resting warmly over hers.

Lisa chuckled nervously. "Honestly? I don't even know where to start. The idea of planning a wedding is... overwhelming."

Harlo smiled. "Then let's keep it simple. It doesn't have to be big or fancy—it just has to feel like us."

Lisa nodded, the tension easing slightly. "Okay. Maybe something small, with just family and close friends. And definitely outside. I want to feel the sun on my skin."

"Sounds perfect," Harlo said.

Telling the Kids
The next step was telling Lisa's children, Emily and Marcus. Though they were both adults now, Lisa was nervous about how they'd react.

She invited them over for dinner, making their favorite dishes to soften the news. As they sat down at the table, Lisa took a deep breath.

"There's something I want to share with you," she began, glancing at Harlo, who gave her an encouraging nod. "Harlo proposed... and I said yes."

For a moment, there was silence. Then Emily broke into a wide grin.

"Mom, that's amazing!" she exclaimed, rushing around the table to hug her.

Marcus was more reserved, his brow furrowed. "You're happy with him?" he asked, his voice serious.

Lisa placed her hand over his. "I am, Marcus. Happier than I've been in a long time. And Harlo's a good man."

After a moment, Marcus nodded. "Then I'm happy for you, too."

Harlo extended his hand, and Marcus shook it firmly. "Welcome to the family," Marcus said, a small smile tugging at his lips.

Navigating Challenges
As they began planning, Lisa quickly realized that keeping the wedding small and simple was easier said than done. The guest list grew longer as Lisa and Harlo both wanted to include people who had supported them during their journey.

"Do we really need to invite Aunt Carol?" Lisa asked one evening, staring at the list. "We haven't spoken in years."

Harlo chuckled. "I think it's okay to focus on the people who are part of our lives now, not just out of obligation."

Lisa nodded, grateful for his perspective. "You're right. Let's keep it intimate."

The other challenge came in the form of finances. Though the community space was thriving, they were careful not to let wedding expenses strain their budget. Lisa and Harlo got creative, enlisting the help of friends for everything from photography to catering.

A Meaningful Venue

After weeks of searching, they found the perfect venue—a local park with a beautiful garden that felt both open and intimate. Standing under the canopy of blooming flowers, Lisa could already imagine herself walking down the makeshift aisle, her heart full of hope and love.

"This is it," she said, turning to Harlo.

He smiled, slipping an arm around her waist. "I couldn't agree more."

A Quiet Moment of Gratitude

One evening, as they worked on handmade decorations for the wedding, Lisa paused, watching Harlo concentrate on tying ribbons around jars for centerpieces.

"Thank you," she said softly.

Harlo looked up, puzzled. "For what?"

"For everything," Lisa said, her voice thick with emotion. "For loving me, for being patient, for helping me believe in this."

Harlo reached across the table, taking her hand. "You don't have to thank me, Lisa. Loving you is the easiest thing I've ever done."

Chapter 28: The Wedding Day

The morning sun filtered through Lisa's bedroom window, casting soft golden light on the dress hanging by the door. A wave of nervous anticipation washed over her as she stretched and took a deep breath. Today was the day.

Emily appeared in the doorway, a steaming cup of tea in hand. "Morning, Mom. You ready to become Mrs. Harlo Reynolds?"

Lisa smiled, her heart fluttering at the sound of the name. "I think so," she said with a chuckle. "Though it still feels surreal."

Emily sat beside her on the bed. "You've come so far, Mom. You deserve this happiness more than anyone I know."

Lisa squeezed her daughter's hand. "Thank you, sweetheart. That means the world to me."

Getting Ready
The house buzzed with activity as friends and family arrived to help Lisa prepare. Her best friend, Denise, worked on her makeup, keeping the look natural and radiant.

"You're glowing, Lisa," Denise said with a smile. "Harlo's a lucky man."

Lisa laughed. "I think we're both pretty lucky."

As the hours ticked by, Lisa slipped into her dress—a simple yet elegant ivory gown that hugged her figure perfectly. When she looked in the mirror, she hardly recognized the woman staring back. Gone was the guarded, uncertain Lisa of the past. In her place stood someone confident, hopeful, and deeply in love.

The Ceremony
The garden was breathtaking. Rows of chairs faced an arch draped with wildflowers, and the warm breeze carried the soft scent of roses. Guests chatted quietly, their excitement palpable.

Harlo stood at the end of the aisle, looking more handsome than ever in a tailored suit. When he saw Lisa step into view, his breath hitched. She was radiant, her smile lighting up the entire garden.

Lisa's arm was hooked through Marcus's, who had insisted on walking her down the aisle. "You look amazing, Mom," he whispered as they approached Harlo.

"Thank you, sweetheart," Lisa replied, her voice thick with emotion.

When she reached Harlo, Marcus gave her hand to him, nodding solemnly. Harlo's eyes never left hers as he took her hands, his grip warm and steady.

Vows from the Heart
The officiant began the ceremony, but Lisa hardly heard the words. Her focus was entirely on Harlo—the way his eyes held hers, the way his smile spoke of quiet joy and unwavering love.

When it was time for the vows, Harlo went first.

"Lisa," he began, his voice steady but full of emotion. "From the moment I met you, I knew you were someone extraordinary. You've shown me the strength of vulnerability, the beauty of resilience, and the power of love. Today, I promise to stand by you, to support you, and to love you with all that I am—for the rest of my life."

Tears streamed down Lisa's face as she prepared to speak her vows.

"Harlo," she began, her voice trembling. "You came into my life when I thought love was impossible, when I was too scared to let anyone in. But you showed me that love isn't something to fear—it's something to cherish. You've been my partner, my anchor, and my greatest joy. Today, I promise to love you fully, to trust you completely, and to walk through life with you, hand in hand."

The crowd sniffled, many wiping away tears.

The Kiss and Celebration
When the officiant pronounced them husband and wife, Harlo didn't hesitate. He pulled Lisa into a tender kiss, their love and commitment radiating to everyone around them.

As they walked back down the aisle together, hand in hand, Lisa felt as though she were floating. This wasn't just a happy ending—it was a new beginning.

The Reception
The reception was a lively affair filled with laughter, dancing, and heartfelt toasts. Emily and Marcus both gave speeches, each expressing their joy and admiration for the couple.

"You've shown us what real love looks like," Emily said, raising her glass. "And I couldn't be happier for you both."

As the evening wound down, Lisa and Harlo stole a quiet moment together under the stars.

"Did you ever think we'd get here?" Lisa asked, leaning against him.

Harlo smiled, wrapping an arm around her. "I always hoped we would. And now that we have, I'm never letting go."

Lisa closed her eyes, feeling the weight of his words. For the first time in her life, she felt truly and deeply loved.

Chapter 29: A New Rhythm

The honeymoon phase, though sweet, didn't come without its adjustments. Married life brought a new rhythm to Lisa and Harlo's relationship—a blend of intimacy, compromise, and the subtle challenges of merging two lives completely.

In the mornings, their routines intertwined in ways both tender and chaotic. Lisa, an early riser, would hum softly as she prepared coffee, while Harlo groggily shuffled into the kitchen, still adjusting to the sunlight.

"You know," Harlo said one morning, squinting at the coffee machine, "I think this thing hates me. Every time I touch it, something spills."

Lisa laughed, handing him a steaming mug. "It's not the machine, Harlo. You're just not awake enough to operate it."

He smirked, taking the cup and wrapping an arm around her waist. "Good thing I've got you to keep me caffeinated and sane."

Learning Each Other's Quirks
As the days turned into weeks, they discovered new quirks about one another. Harlo had a habit of leaving his tools scattered around the house after working on a project, much to Lisa's chagrin.

"Why is there a hammer on the dining table?" she asked one evening, holding it up with an amused expression.

Harlo shrugged sheepishly. "I was fixing the chair earlier and got distracted."

Lisa shook her head, laughing. "You're lucky I love you. But this hammer is going in the toolbox."

On the flip side, Lisa's meticulous organization occasionally drove Harlo up the wall. One afternoon, he searched the kitchen for twenty minutes before realizing she'd rearranged the pantry again.

"Babe, where's the peanut butter?" he called out.

"Top shelf, left corner," Lisa replied from the living room.

Harlo sighed, grinning despite himself. "Do you have a map for this pantry, or should I just start labeling things?"

The Quiet Moments
But amidst the humorous adjustments were moments of profound connection. On lazy Sunday afternoons, they would curl up on the couch together, Lisa's head resting on Harlo's chest as he read aloud from one of his favorite books.

"Your voice is so calming," Lisa said one day, her eyes half-closed.

"Is that your way of saying I'm putting you to sleep?" Harlo teased, earning a playful slap on his arm.

"No," Lisa replied with a smile. "It's my way of saying I could listen to you forever."

Harlo kissed the top of her head. "Forever sounds pretty good to me."

Navigating Challenges
Not everything was easy. They occasionally clashed over decisions—what to spend money on, how to balance time between their individual projects and shared goals.

One evening, Lisa came home visibly stressed after a particularly demanding day at the community space.

"Everything okay?" Harlo asked, concern etched on his face.

She sighed, sinking into the couch. "It's just a lot sometimes. I feel like there's always more to do, and I don't want to let anyone down."

Harlo sat beside her, taking her hands in his. "You don't have to carry it all on your own, Lisa. Let me help. We're a team now, remember?"

His words brought tears to her eyes, and she nodded. "Thank you, Harlo. I don't know what I'd do without you."

A Deeper Love
As they settled into their life together, Lisa began to notice how their love deepened in small, meaningful ways. It wasn't always grand gestures or romantic surprises—sometimes it was in the way Harlo would warm her coat before she went out on chilly mornings, or the way Lisa would leave little notes in his lunchbox, reminding him how much he meant to her.

One night, as they lay in bed, Lisa turned to Harlo.

"Do you ever wonder how we got here?" she asked softly.

Harlo smiled, brushing a strand of hair from her face. "All the time. And every time, I'm grateful we did."

Lisa nestled closer to him, feeling the steady rhythm of his heartbeat. For the first time in her life, she felt completely at home—not just in her house, but in her heart.